THE WONDERFUL WIZARD OF OZ

VOL. 1

ADAPTED FROM THE NOVEL BY L. FRANK BAUM

Writer: ERIC SHANOWER
Artist: SKOTTIE YOUNG
Colorist: JEAN-FRANCOIS BEAULIEU
Letterer: JEFF ECKLEBERRY

Assistant Editors: LAUREN SANKOVITCH & LAUREN HENRY
Associate Editor: NATE COSBY
Senior Editor: RALPH MACCHIO

Special Thanks to Chris Allo, Rich Ginter, Jeff Suter & Jim Nausedas
Collection Editor: MARK D. BEAZLEY
Assistant Editors: NELSON RIBEIRO & ALEX STARBUCK
Editor, Special Projects: JENNIFER GRÜNWALD
Senior Editor, Special Projects: JEFF YOUNGQUIST
SVP of Print & Digital Publishing Sales: DAVID GABRIEL
Production: JERRY KALINOWSKI
Book Design: SPRING HOTELING

Editor in Chief: AXEL ALONSO
Chief Creative Officer: JOE QUESADA
Publisher: DAN BUCKLEY
Executive Producer: ALAN FINE

MARVEL

visit us at www.abdopublishing.com

Reinforced library bound edition published in 2014 by Spotlight, a division of the ABDO Group, PO Box 398166, Minneapolis, Minnesota 55439. Spotlight produces high-quality reinforced library bound editions for schools and libraries. Published by agreement with Marvel Characters, Inc.

Printed in the United States of America, North Mankato, Minnesota.
102013
012014
This book contains at least 10% recycled materials.

MARVEL
Marvel.com

Library of Congress Cataloging-in-Publication Data

Shanower, Eric.
The wonderful Wizard of Oz / adapted from the novel by L. Frank Baum ; writer: Eric Shanower ; artist: Skottie Young. -- Reinforced library bound edition.
pages cm
"Marvel."
Summary: An eight-volume, graphic novel adaptation of L. Frank Baum's tales of Dorothy, a little girl from Kansas who is blown by a storm to the magical land of Oz, where she has amazing adventures while trying to get home.
ISBN 978-1-61479-226-0 (vol. 1) -- ISBN 978-1-61479-227-7 (vol. 2) -- ISBN 978-1-61479-228-4 (vol. 3) -- ISBN 978-1-61479-229-1 (vol. 4) -- ISBN 978-1-61479-230-7 (vol. 5) -- ISBN 978-1-61479-231-4 (vol. 6) -- ISBN 978-1-61479-232-1 (vol. 7) -- ISBN 978-1-61479-233-8 (vol. 8)
1. Graphic novels. [1. Graphic novels. 2. Fantasy.] I. Young, Skottie, illustrator. II. Baum, L. Frank (Lyman Frank), 1856-1919. III. Title.
PZ7.7.S453Won 2014
741.5'973--dc23

2013029128

Spotlight

All Spotlight books are reinforced library binding and manufactured in the United States of America.

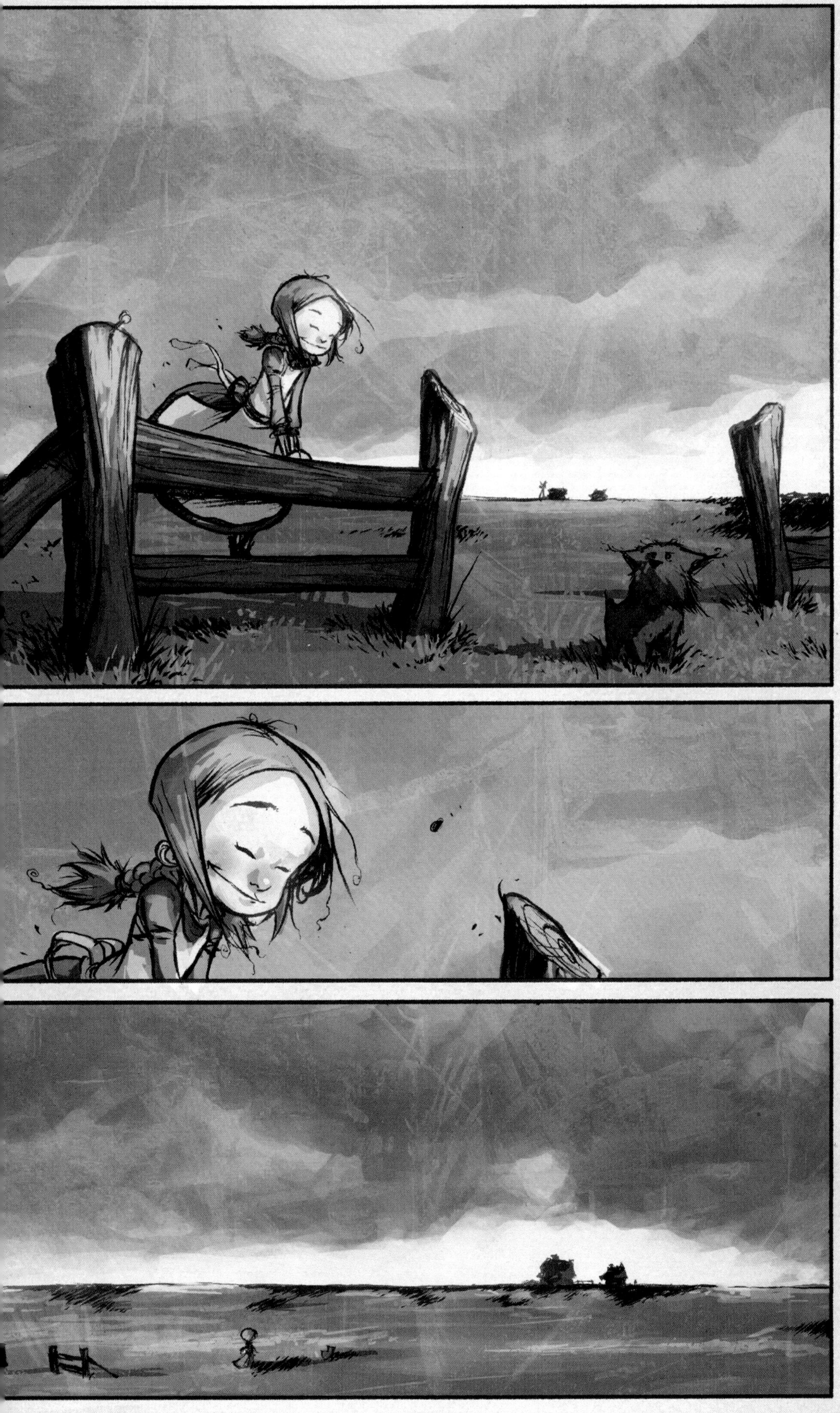

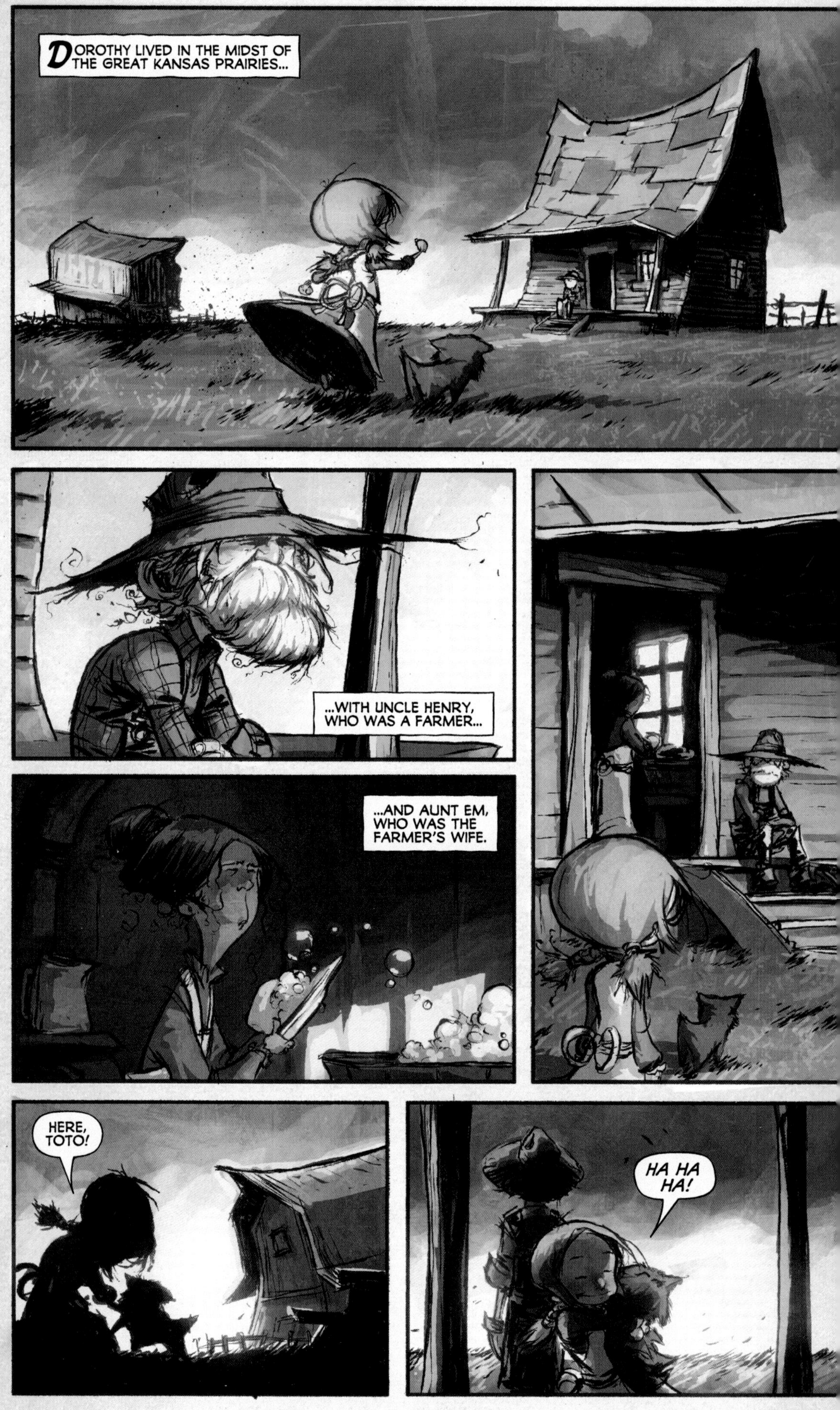
DOROTHY LIVED IN THE MIDST OF THE GREAT KANSAS PRAIRIES...
...WITH UNCLE HENRY, WHO WAS A FARMER...
...AND AUNT EM, WHO WAS THE FARMER'S WIFE.
HERE, TOTO!
HA HA HA!

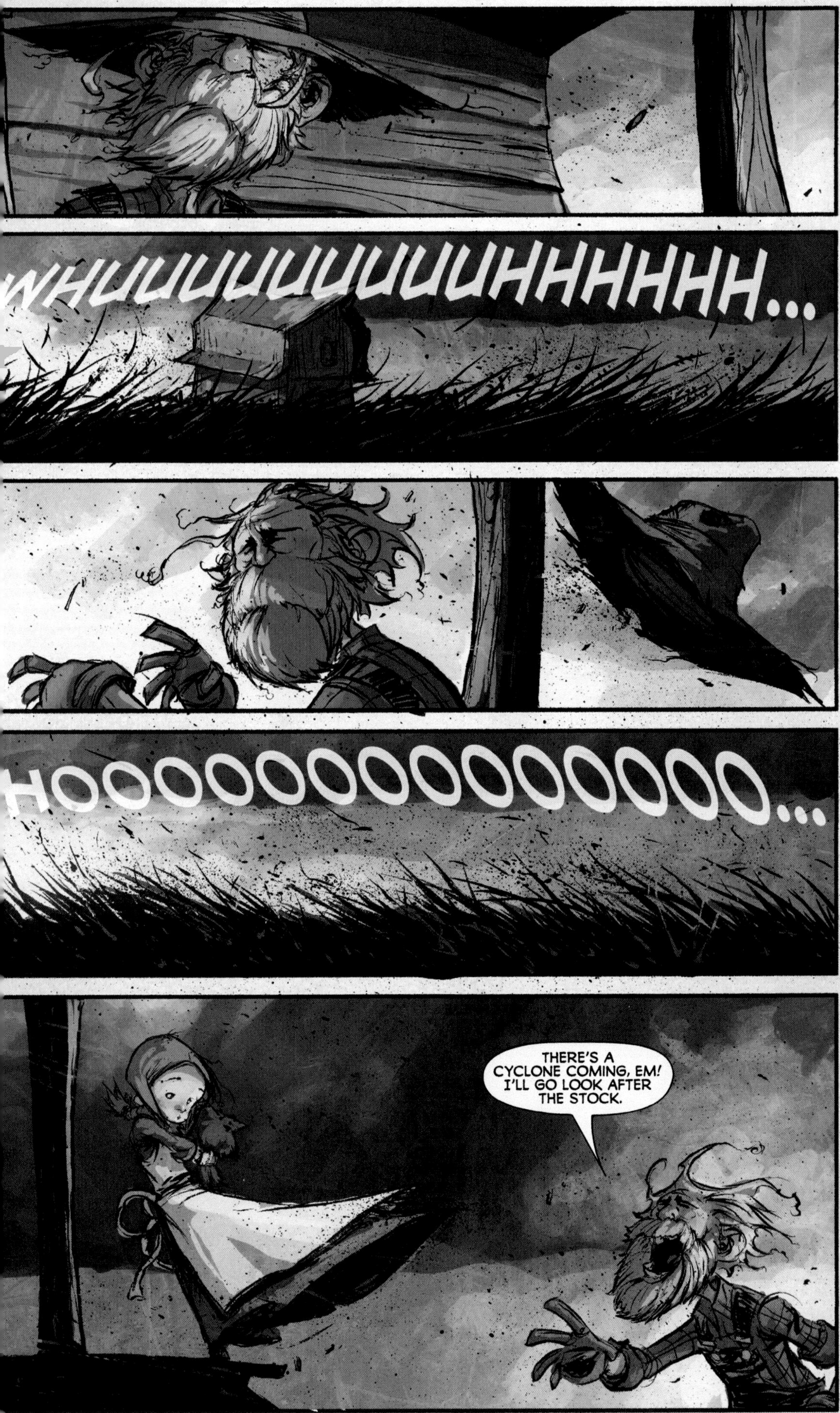
WHUUUUUUUUUUUHHHHHH...
HOOOOOOOOOOOOOOO...
THERE'S A CYCLONE COMING, EM! I'LL GO LOOK AFTER THE STOCK.

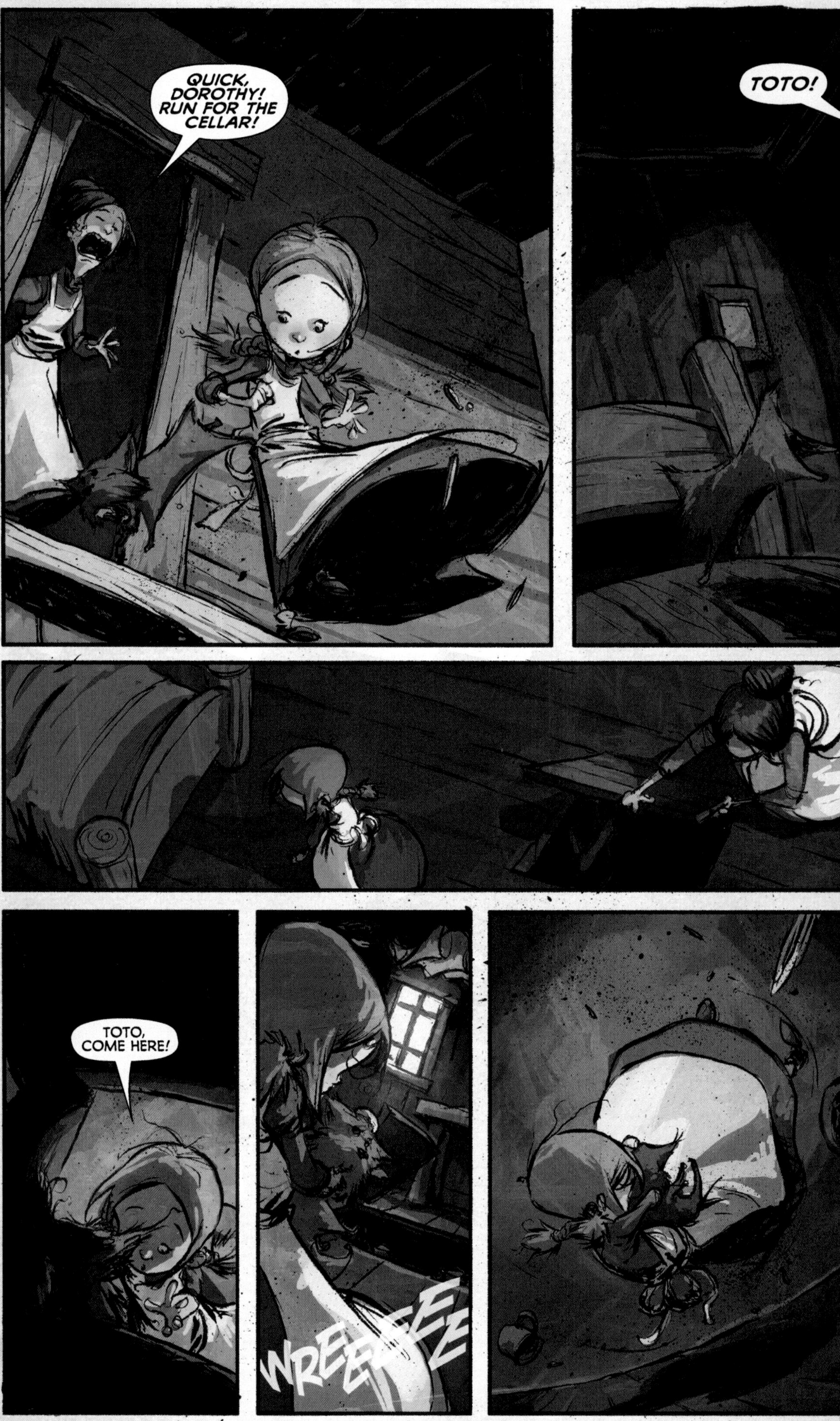
QUICK, DOROTHY! RUN FOR THE CELLAR!
TOTO!
TOTO, COME HERE!
WREEEEEE

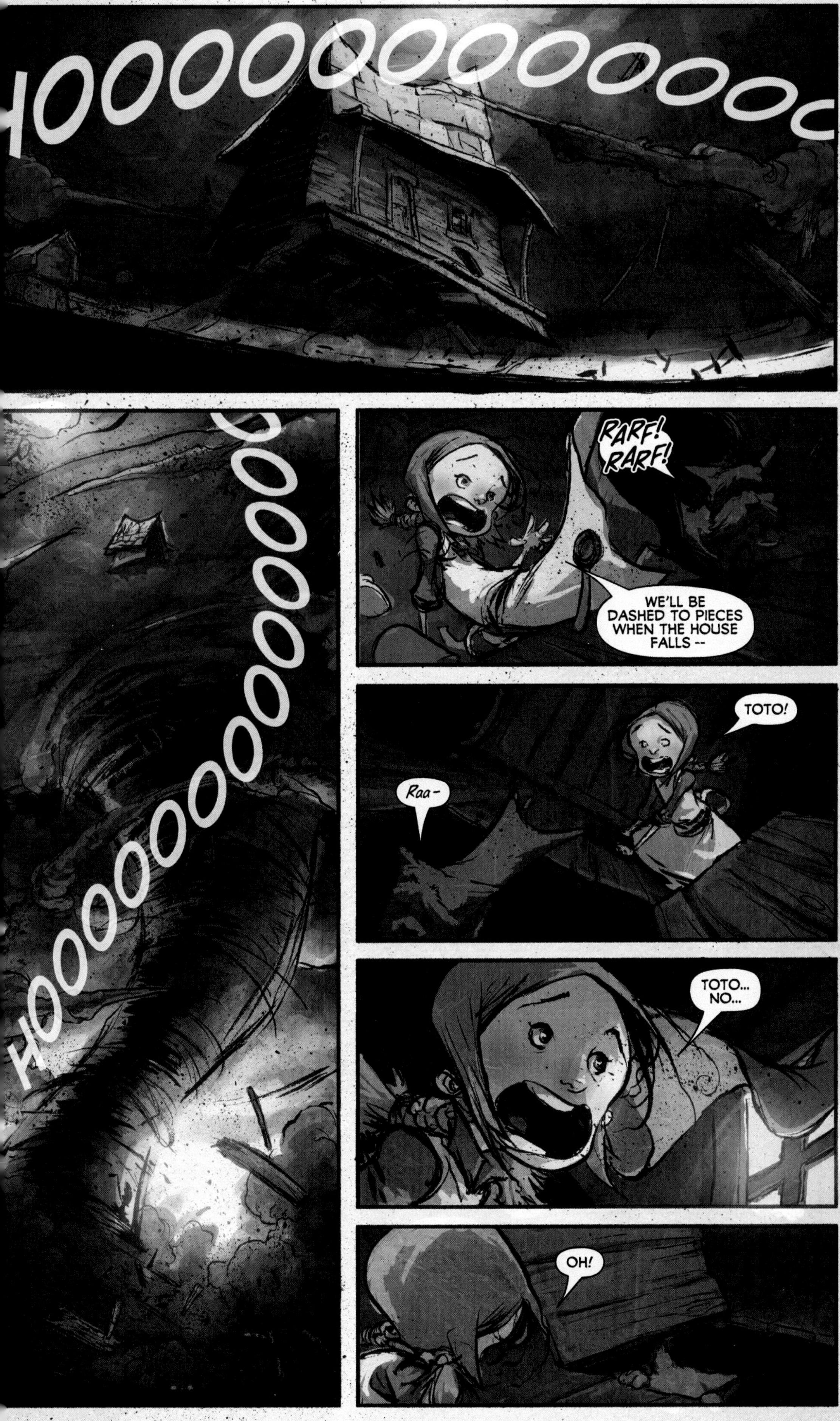
HOOOOOOOOOOOOOO
OOOOOOOOOOOO
HOOOOOOO
RARF! RARF!
WE'LL BE DASHED TO PIECES WHEN THE HOUSE FALLS --
TOTO!
Raa-
TOTO... NO...
OH!

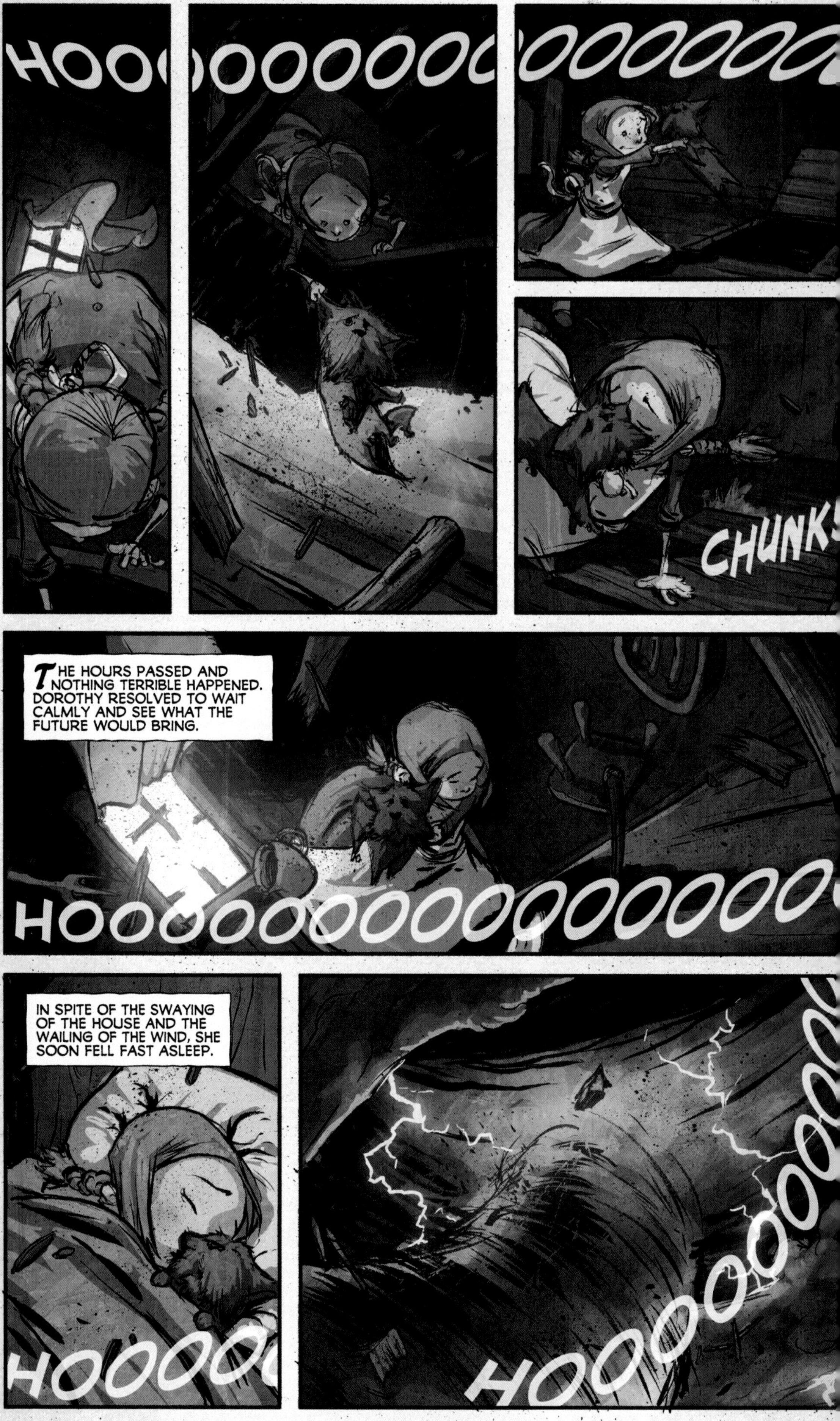
HOOOOOOOOOOOOOOOOOOOO
CHUNK!
THE HOURS PASSED AND NOTHING TERRIBLE HAPPENED. DOROTHY RESOLVED TO WAIT CALMLY AND SEE WHAT THE FUTURE WOULD BRING.
HOOOOOOOOOOOOOOOOO
IN SPITE OF THE SWAYING OF THE HOUSE AND THE WAILING OF THE WIND, SHE SOON FELL FAST ASLEEP.
HOOOOO
HOOOOOOOOOOOOO

WHUNK

Whiiii...

OH!

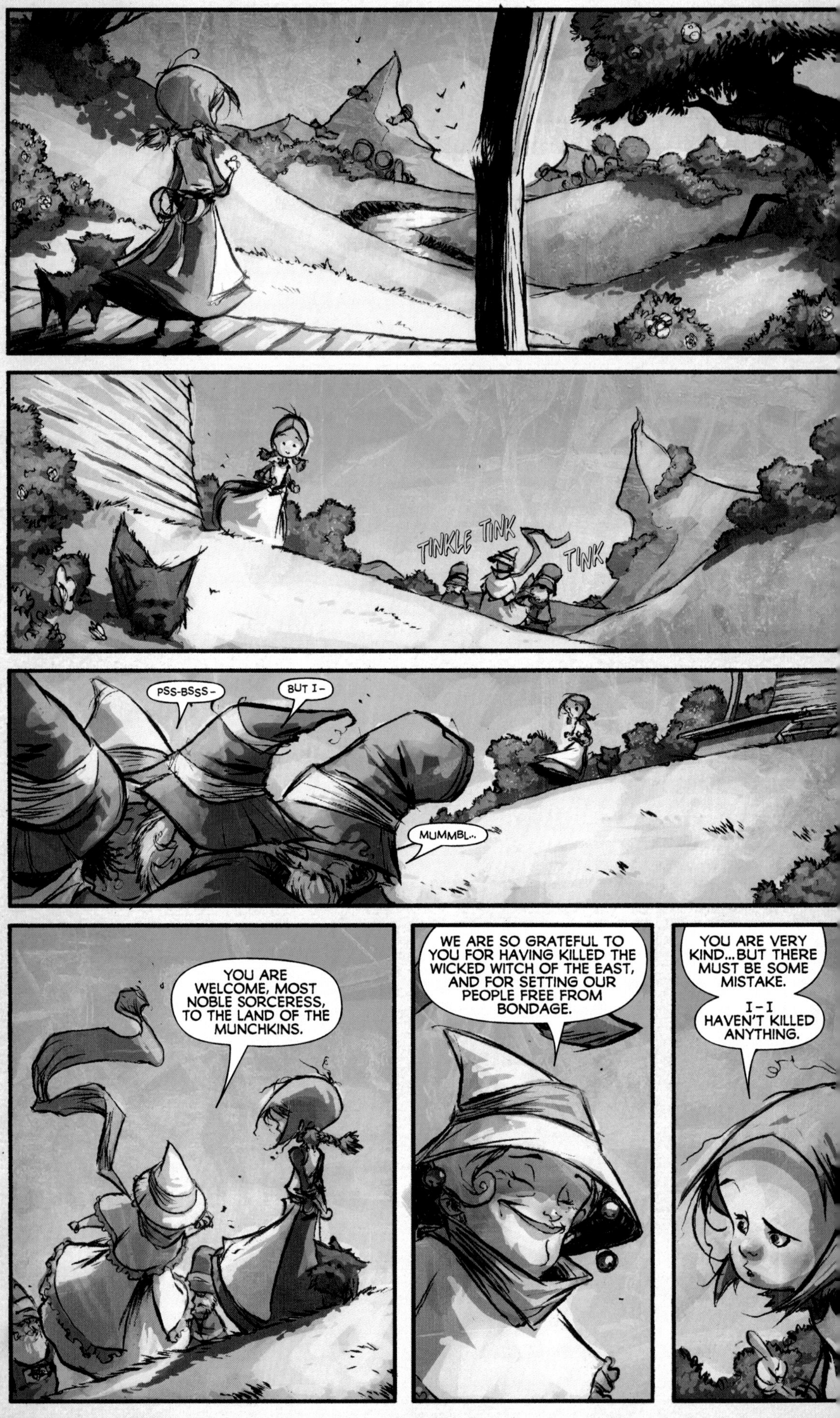
TINKLE TINK
TINK
PSS-BSSS -
BUT I-
MUMMBL..
YOU ARE WELCOME, MOST NOBLE SORCERESS, TO THE LAND OF THE MUNCHKINS.
WE ARE SO GRATEFUL TO YOU FOR HAVING KILLED THE WICKED WITCH OF THE EAST, AND FOR SETTING OUR PEOPLE FREE FROM BONDAGE.
YOU ARE VERY KIND...BUT THERE MUST BE SOME MISTAKE.
I - I HAVEN'T KILLED ANYTHING.

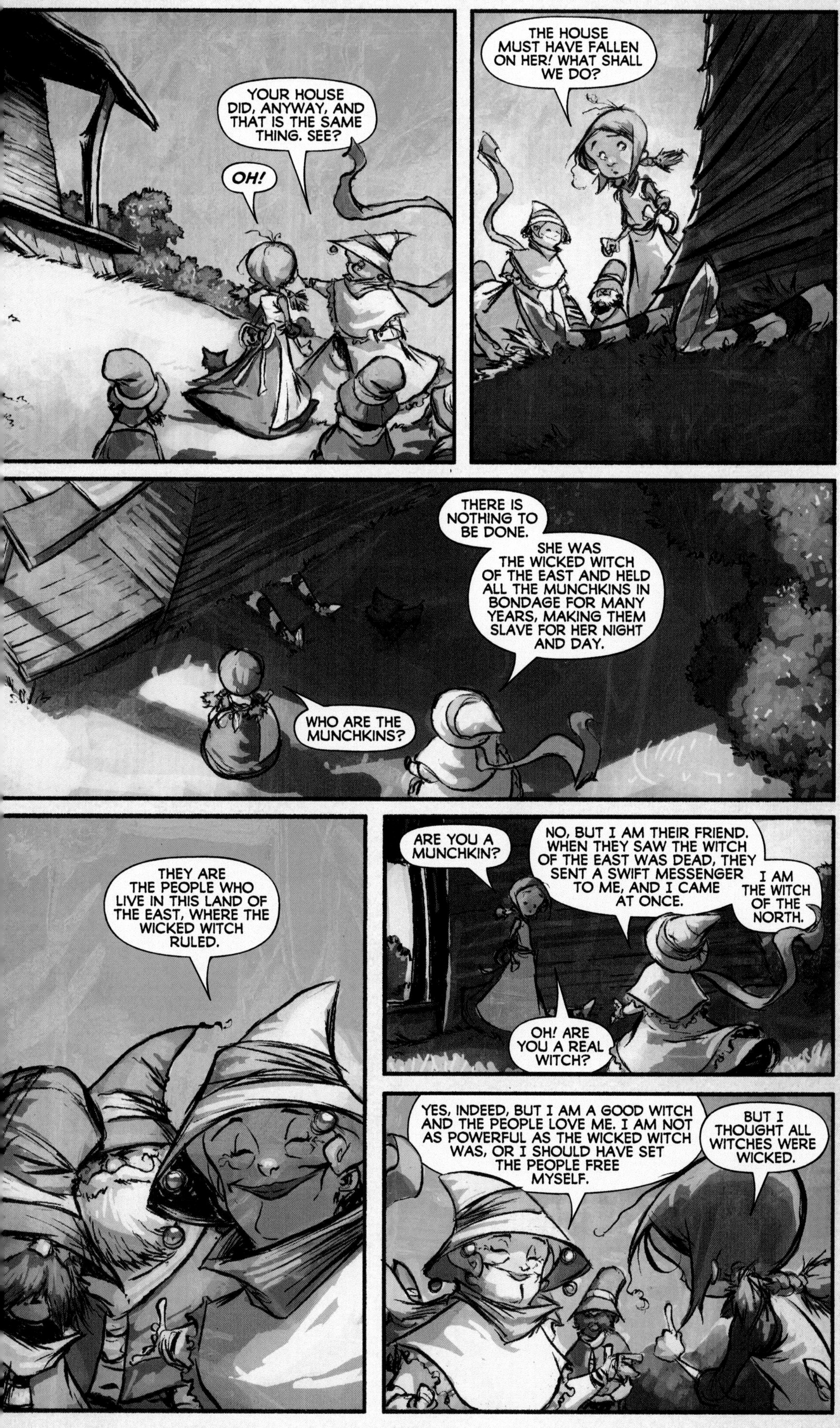
YOUR HOUSE DID, ANYWAY, AND THAT IS THE SAME THING. SEE?
OH!
THE HOUSE MUST HAVE FALLEN ON HER! WHAT SHALL WE DO?
THERE IS NOTHING TO BE DONE.
SHE WAS THE WICKED WITCH OF THE EAST AND HELD ALL THE MUNCHKINS IN BONDAGE FOR MANY YEARS, MAKING THEM SLAVE FOR HER NIGHT AND DAY.
WHO ARE THE MUNCHKINS?
THEY ARE THE PEOPLE WHO LIVE IN THIS LAND OF THE EAST, WHERE THE WICKED WITCH RULED.
ARE YOU A MUNCHKIN?
NO, BUT I AM THEIR FRIEND. WHEN THEY SAW THE WITCH OF THE EAST WAS DEAD, THEY SENT A SWIFT MESSENGER TO ME, AND I CAME AT ONCE.
I AM THE WITCH OF THE NORTH.
OH! ARE YOU A REAL WITCH?
YES, INDEED, BUT I AM A GOOD WITCH AND THE PEOPLE LOVE ME. I AM NOT AS POWERFUL AS THE WICKED WITCH WAS, OR I SHOULD HAVE SET THE PEOPLE FREE MYSELF.
BUT I THOUGHT ALL WITCHES WERE WICKED.

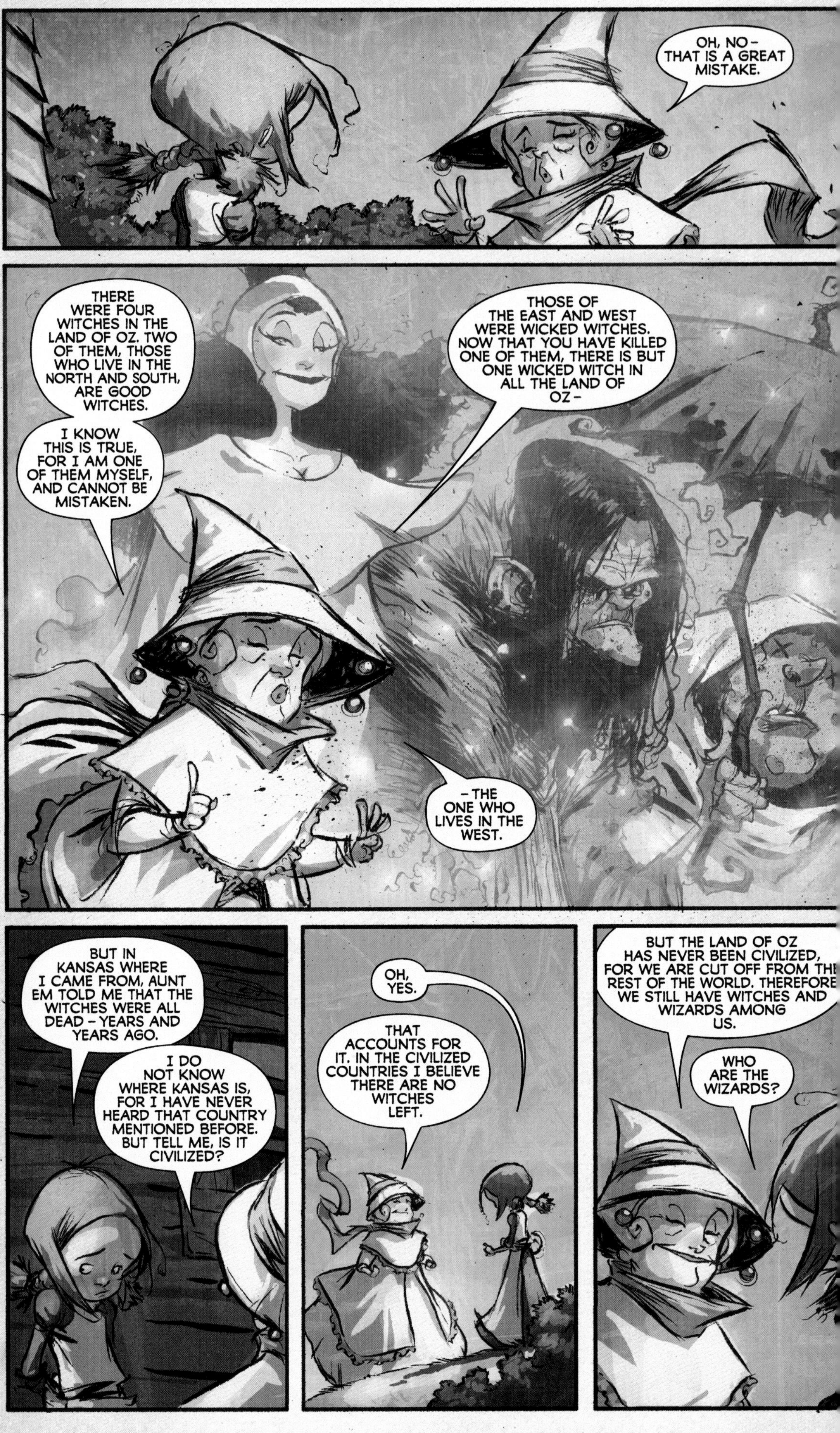
OH, NO– THAT IS A GREAT MISTAKE.
THERE WERE FOUR WITCHES IN THE LAND OF OZ. TWO OF THEM, THOSE WHO LIVE IN THE NORTH AND SOUTH, ARE GOOD WITCHES.
I KNOW THIS IS TRUE, FOR I AM ONE OF THEM MYSELF, AND CANNOT BE MISTAKEN.
THOSE OF THE EAST AND WEST WERE WICKED WITCHES. NOW THAT YOU HAVE KILLED ONE OF THEM, THERE IS BUT ONE WICKED WITCH IN ALL THE LAND OF OZ–
–THE ONE WHO LIVES IN THE WEST.
BUT IN KANSAS WHERE I CAME FROM, AUNT EM TOLD ME THAT THE WITCHES WERE ALL DEAD – YEARS AND YEARS AGO.
I DO NOT KNOW WHERE KANSAS IS, FOR I HAVE NEVER HEARD THAT COUNTRY MENTIONED BEFORE. BUT TELL ME, IS IT CIVILIZED?
OH, YES.
THAT ACCOUNTS FOR IT. IN THE CIVILIZED COUNTRIES I BELIEVE THERE ARE NO WITCHES LEFT.
BUT THE LAND OF OZ HAS NEVER BEEN CIVILIZED, FOR WE ARE CUT OFF FROM THE REST OF THE WORLD. THEREFORE WE STILL HAVE WITCHES AND WIZARDS AMONG US.
WHO ARE THE WIZARDS?

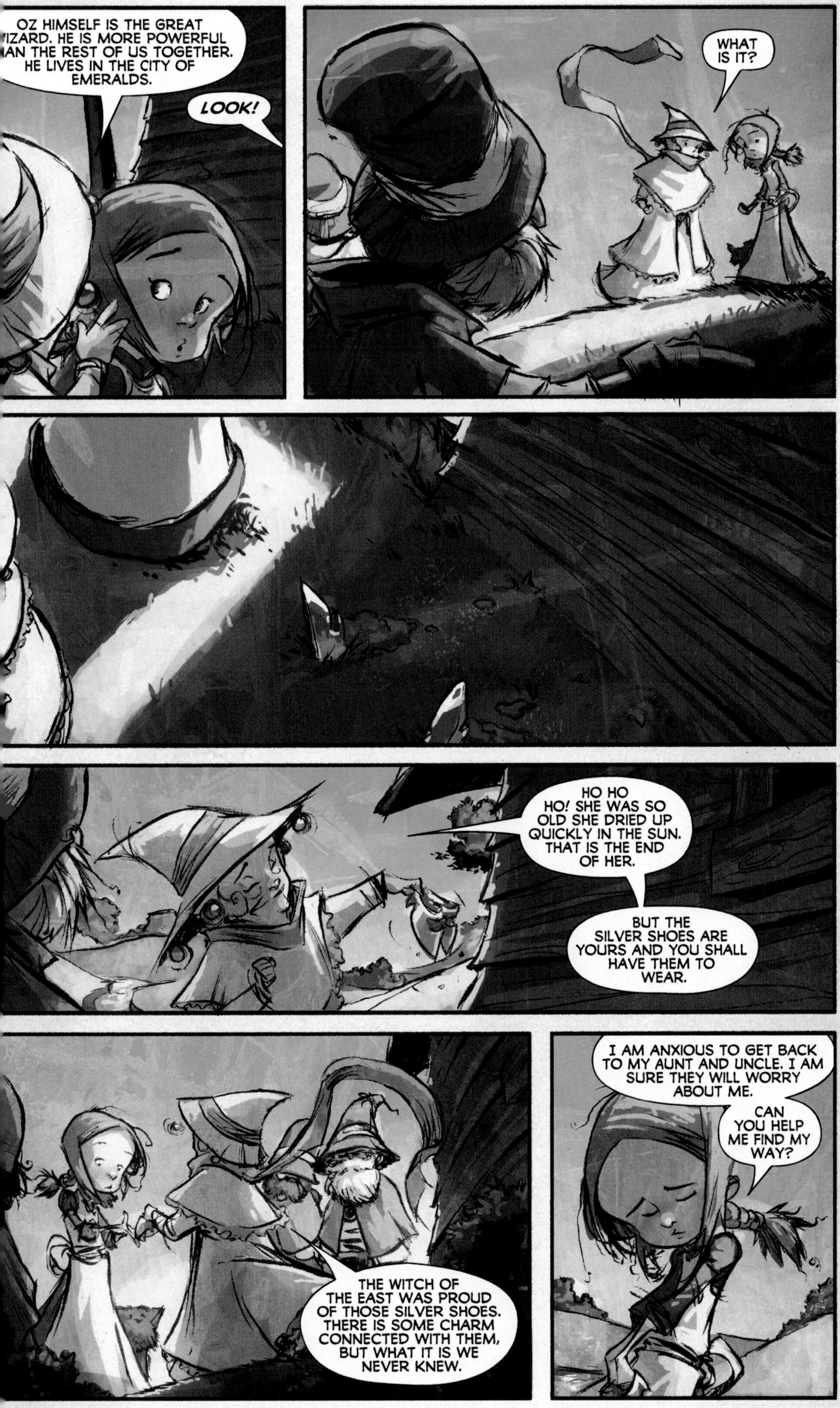
OZ HIMSELF IS THE GREAT WIZARD. HE IS MORE POWERFUL THAN THE REST OF US TOGETHER. HE LIVES IN THE CITY OF EMERALDS.
LOOK!
WHAT IS IT?
HO HO HO! SHE WAS SO OLD SHE DRIED UP QUICKLY IN THE SUN. THAT IS THE END OF HER.
BUT THE SILVER SHOES ARE YOURS AND YOU SHALL HAVE THEM TO WEAR.
THE WITCH OF THE EAST WAS PROUD OF THOSE SILVER SHOES. THERE IS SOME CHARM CONNECTED WITH THEM, BUT WHAT IT IS WE NEVER KNEW.
I AM ANXIOUS TO GET BACK TO MY AUNT AND UNCLE. I AM SURE THEY WILL WORRY ABOUT ME.
CAN YOU HELP ME FIND MY WAY?

AT THE EAST, NOT FAR FROM HERE, THERE IS A GREAT DESERT. *NONE* COULD LIVE TO CROSS IT.

IT IS THE SAME AT THE SOUTH, FOR I HAVE BEEN THERE AND SEEN IT. THE SOUTH IS THE COUNTRY OF THE QUADLINGS.

I AM TOLD IT IS THE SAME IN THE WEST. THAT COUNTRY WHERE THE WINKIES LIV IS RULED BY THE WICKE WITCH OF THE WEST, WH WOULD MAKE YOU HEI SLAVE IF YOU PASSED HER WAY.

THE NORTH IS MY HOME AND AT ITS EDGE IS THE SAME GREAT DESERT THAT SURROUNDS THIS LAND OF OZ.

I'M AFRAID, MY DEAR, YOU'LL HAVE TO LIVE WITH US.

*D*OROTHY BEGAN TO SOB, FOR SHE FELT LONELY AMONG ALL THESE STRANGE PEOPLE.

THE WOMAN TOOK OFF HER CAP AND BALANCED IT ON THE END OF HER NOSE

TINKLE

ONE, TWO, THREE!

TINKLE

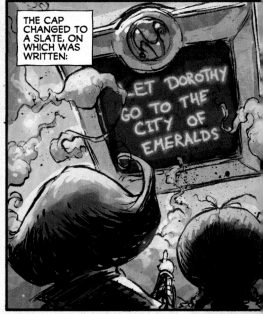

THE CAP CHANGED TO A SLATE, ON WHICH WAS WRITTEN:

ET DOROTHY GO TO THE CITY OF EMERALDS

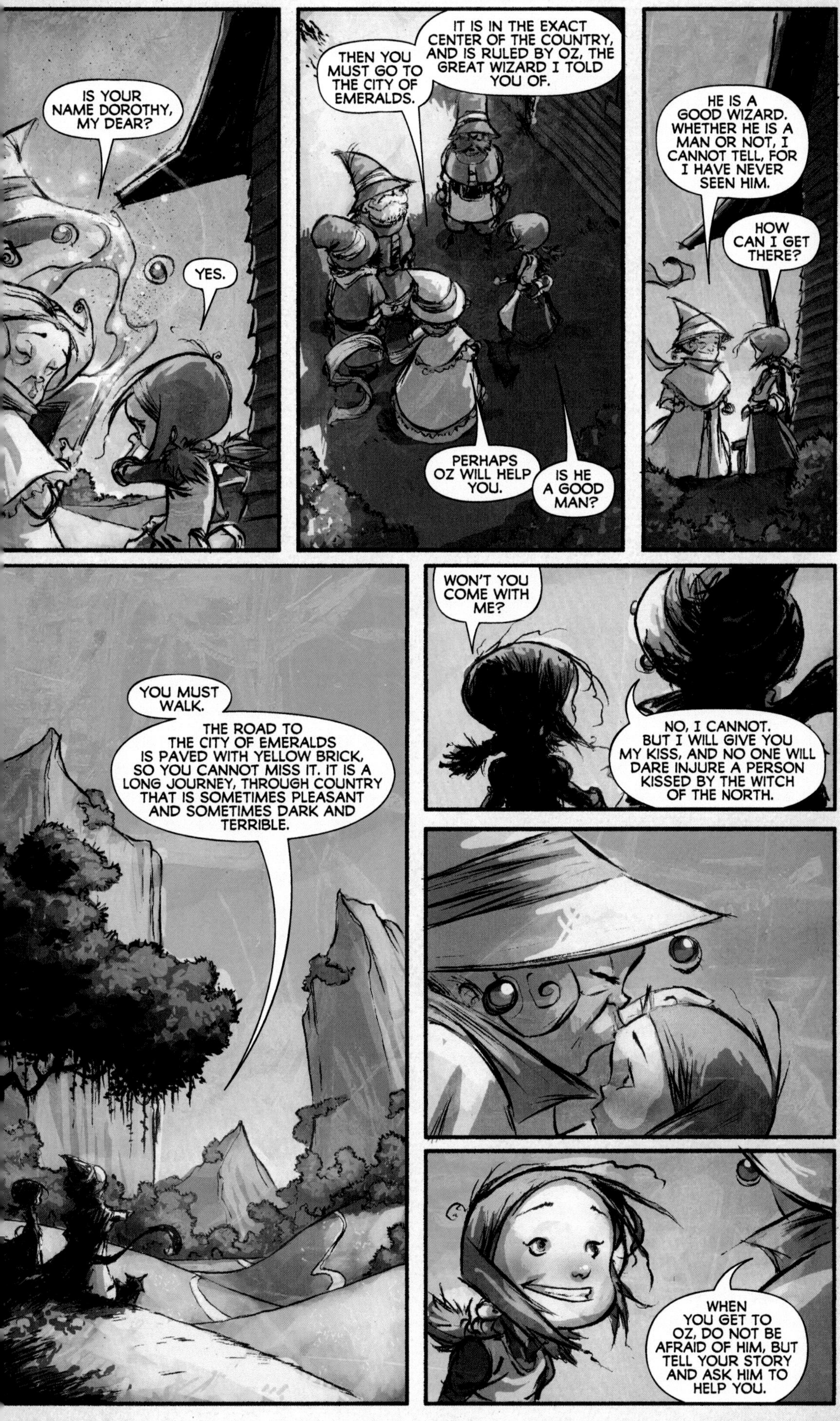
IS YOUR NAME DOROTHY, MY DEAR?
YES.
THEN YOU MUST GO TO THE CITY OF EMERALDS.
IT IS IN THE EXACT CENTER OF THE COUNTRY, AND IS RULED BY OZ, THE GREAT WIZARD I TOLD YOU OF.
PERHAPS OZ WILL HELP YOU.
IS HE A GOOD MAN?
HE IS A GOOD WIZARD. WHETHER HE IS A MAN OR NOT, I CANNOT TELL, FOR I HAVE NEVER SEEN HIM.
HOW CAN I GET THERE?
YOU MUST WALK.
THE ROAD TO THE CITY OF EMERALDS IS PAVED WITH YELLOW BRICK, SO YOU CANNOT MISS IT. IT IS A LONG JOURNEY, THROUGH COUNTRY THAT IS SOMETIMES PLEASANT AND SOMETIMES DARK AND TERRIBLE.
WON'T YOU COME WITH ME?
NO, I CANNOT. BUT I WILL GIVE YOU MY KISS, AND NO ONE WILL DARE INJURE A PERSON KISSED BY THE WITCH OF THE NORTH.
WHEN YOU GET TO OZ, DO NOT BE AFRAID OF HIM, BUT TELL YOUR STORY AND ASK HIM TO HELP YOU.

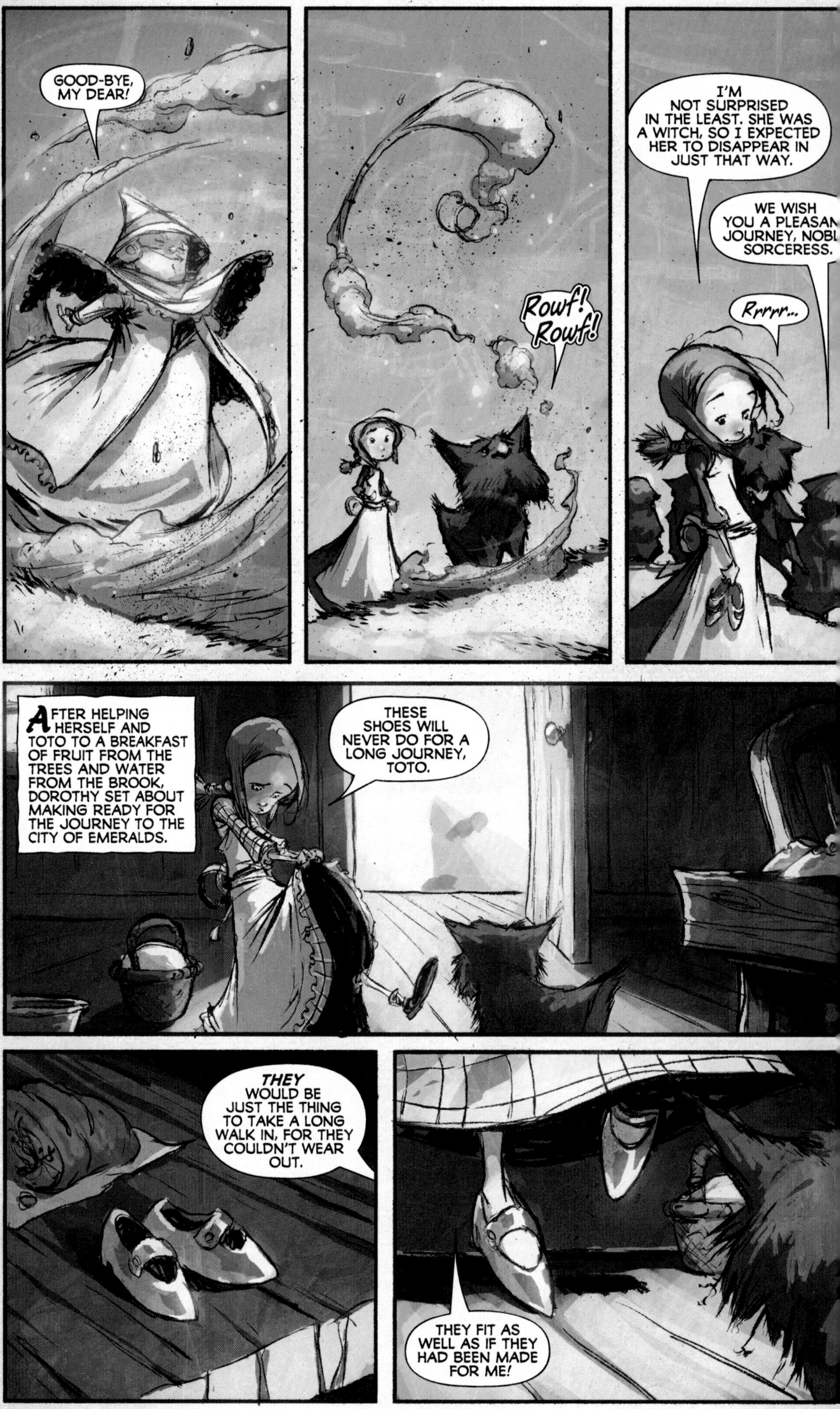
GOOD-BYE, MY DEAR!
Rowf! Rowf!
I'M NOT SURPRISED IN THE LEAST. SHE WAS A WITCH, SO I EXPECTED HER TO DISAPPEAR IN JUST THAT WAY.
WE WISH YOU A PLEASAN JOURNEY, NOBL SORCERESS.
Rrrrr...
AFTER HELPING HERSELF AND TOTO TO A BREAKFAST OF FRUIT FROM THE TREES AND WATER FROM THE BROOK, DOROTHY SET ABOUT MAKING READY FOR THE JOURNEY TO THE CITY OF EMERALDS.
THESE SHOES WILL NEVER DO FOR A LONG JOURNEY, TOTO.
THEY WOULD BE JUST THE THING TO TAKE A LONG WALK IN, FOR THEY COULDN'T WEAR OUT.
THEY FIT AS WELL AS IF THEY HAD BEEN MADE FOR ME!

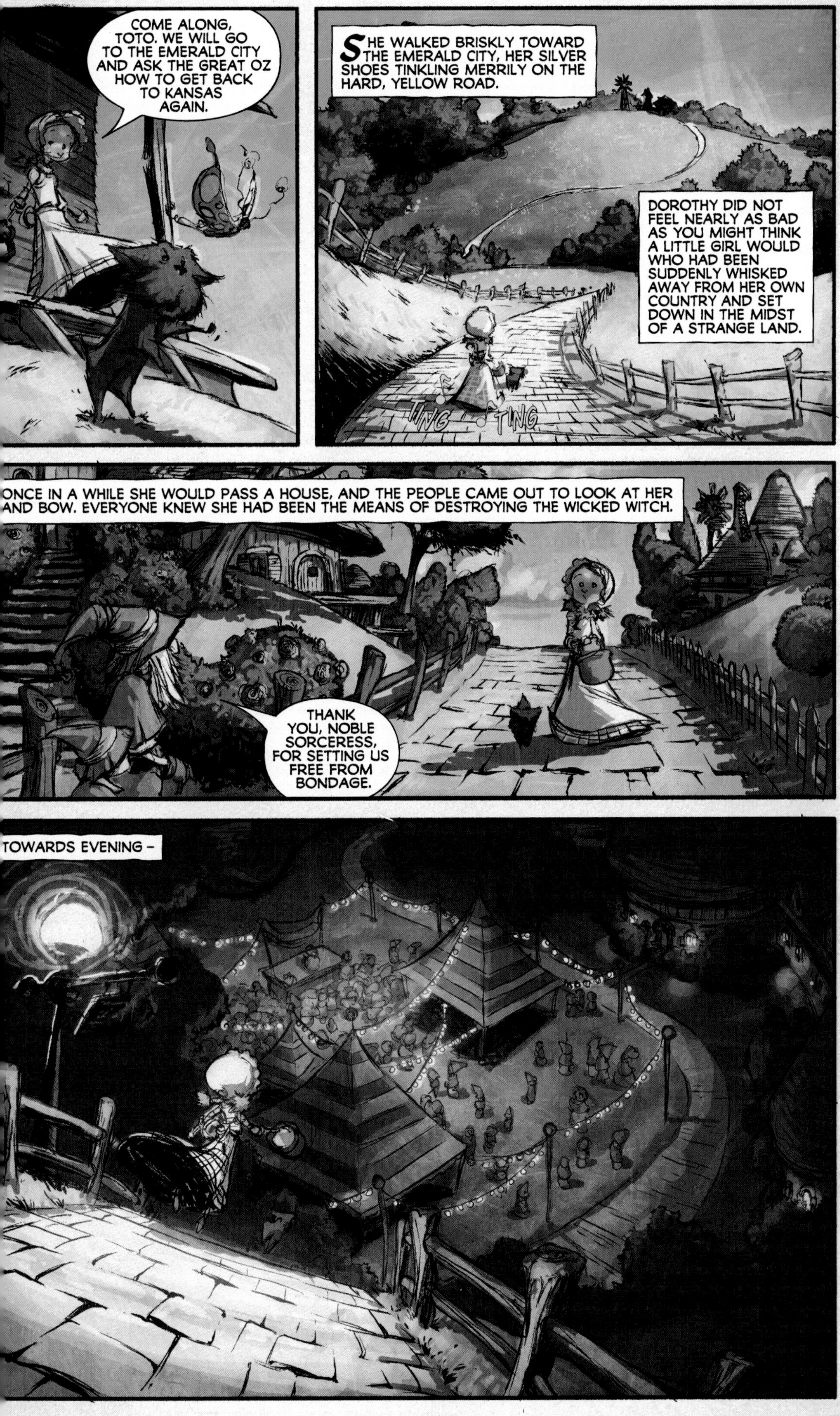
COME ALONG, TOTO. WE WILL GO TO THE EMERALD CITY AND ASK THE GREAT OZ HOW TO GET BACK TO KANSAS AGAIN.
SHE WALKED BRISKLY TOWARD THE EMERALD CITY, HER SILVER SHOES TINKLING MERRILY ON THE HARD, YELLOW ROAD.
DOROTHY DID NOT FEEL NEARLY AS BAD AS YOU MIGHT THINK A LITTLE GIRL WOULD WHO HAD BEEN SUDDENLY WHISKED AWAY FROM HER OWN COUNTRY AND SET DOWN IN THE MIDST OF A STRANGE LAND.
TING TING
ONCE IN A WHILE SHE WOULD PASS A HOUSE, AND THE PEOPLE CAME OUT TO LOOK AT HER AND BOW. EVERYONE KNEW SHE HAD BEEN THE MEANS OF DESTROYING THE WICKED WITCH.
THANK YOU, NOBLE SORCERESS, FOR SETTING US FREE FROM BONDAGE.
TOWARDS EVENING –

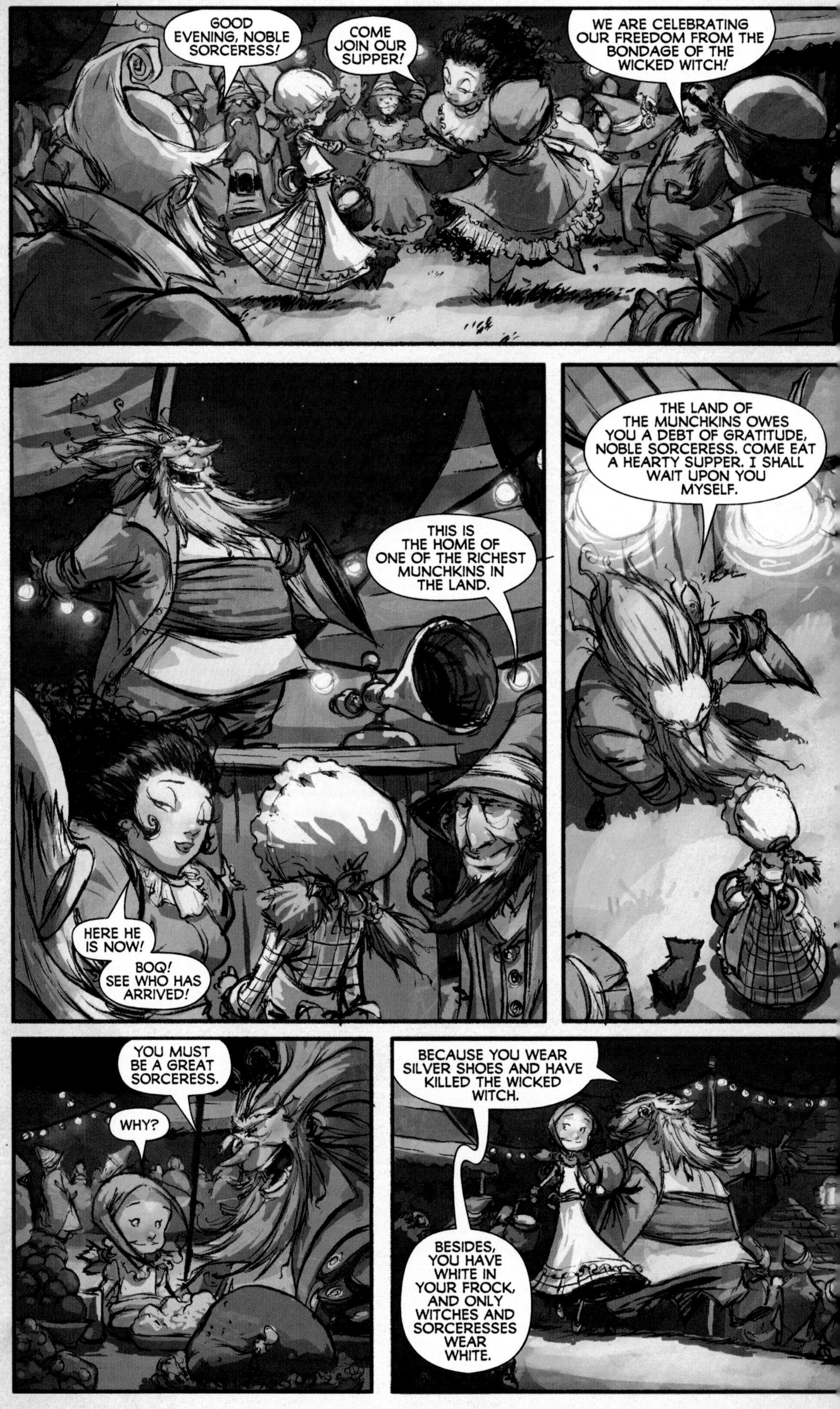
GOOD EVENING, NOBLE SORCERESS!
COME JOIN OUR SUPPER!
WE ARE CELEBRATING OUR FREEDOM FROM THE BONDAGE OF THE WICKED WITCH!
THIS IS THE HOME OF ONE OF THE RICHEST MUNCHKINS IN THE LAND.
HERE HE IS NOW!
BOQ! SEE WHO HAS ARRIVED!
THE LAND OF THE MUNCHKINS OWES YOU A DEBT OF GRATITUDE, NOBLE SORCERESS. COME EAT A HEARTY SUPPER. I SHALL WAIT UPON YOU MYSELF.
YOU MUST BE A GREAT SORCERESS.
WHY?
BECAUSE YOU WEAR SILVER SHOES AND HAVE KILLED THE WICKED WITCH.
BESIDES, YOU HAVE WHITE IN YOUR FROCK, AND ONLY WITCHES AND SORCERESSES WEAR WHITE.

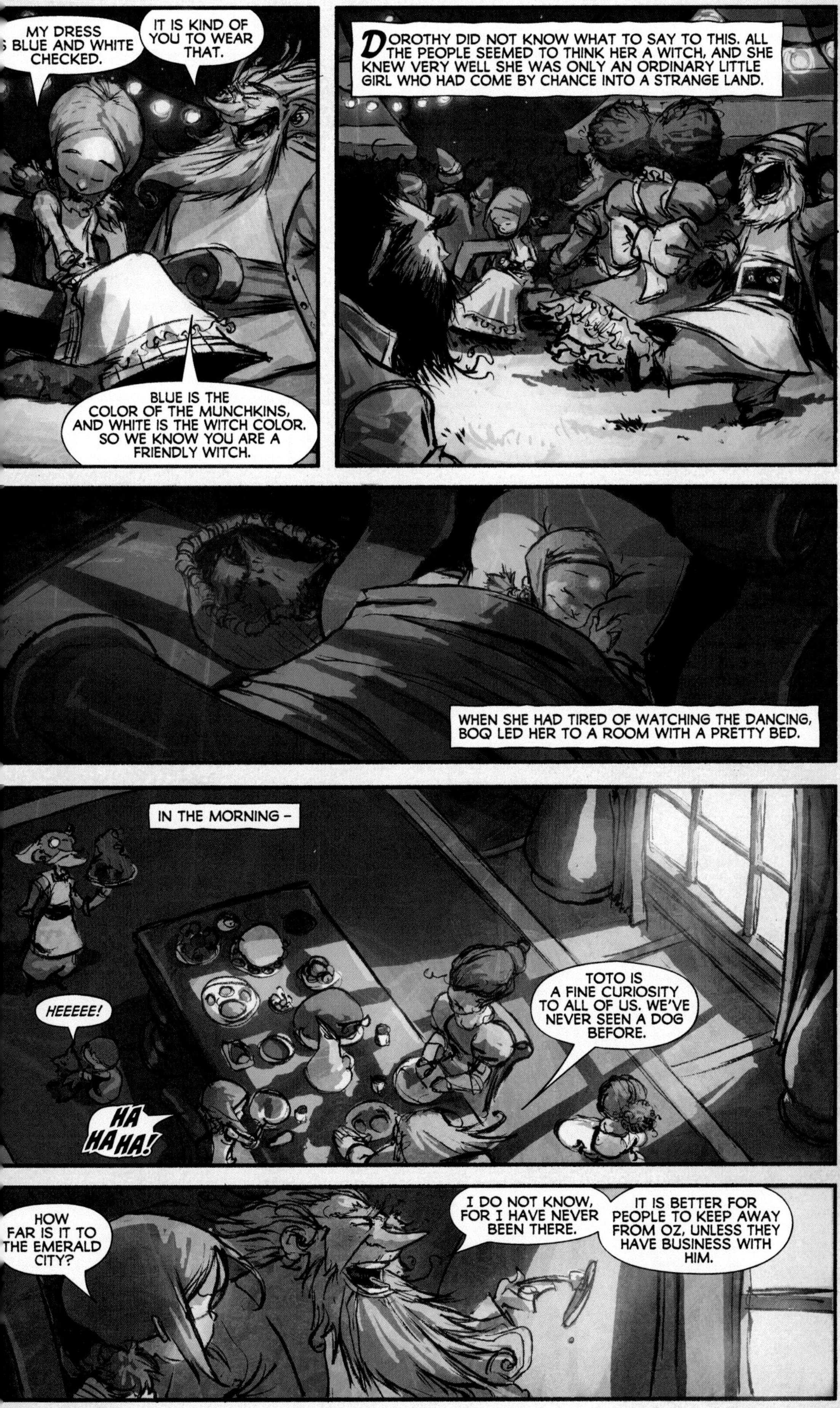
MY DRESS
S BLUE AND WHITE CHECKED.
IT IS KIND OF YOU TO WEAR THAT.
BLUE IS THE COLOR OF THE MUNCHKINS, AND WHITE IS THE WITCH COLOR. SO WE KNOW YOU ARE A FRIENDLY WITCH.
DOROTHY DID NOT KNOW WHAT TO SAY TO THIS. ALL THE PEOPLE SEEMED TO THINK HER A WITCH, AND SHE KNEW VERY WELL SHE WAS ONLY AN ORDINARY LITTLE GIRL WHO HAD COME BY CHANCE INTO A STRANGE LAND.
WHEN SHE HAD TIRED OF WATCHING THE DANCING, BOQ LED HER TO A ROOM WITH A PRETTY BED.
IN THE MORNING –
HEEEEE!
HA HA HA!
TOTO IS A FINE CURIOSITY TO ALL OF US. WE'VE NEVER SEEN A DOG BEFORE.
HOW FAR IS IT TO THE EMERALD CITY?
I DO NOT KNOW, FOR I HAVE NEVER BEEN THERE.
IT IS BETTER FOR PEOPLE TO KEEP AWAY FROM OZ, UNLESS THEY HAVE BUSINESS WITH HIM.

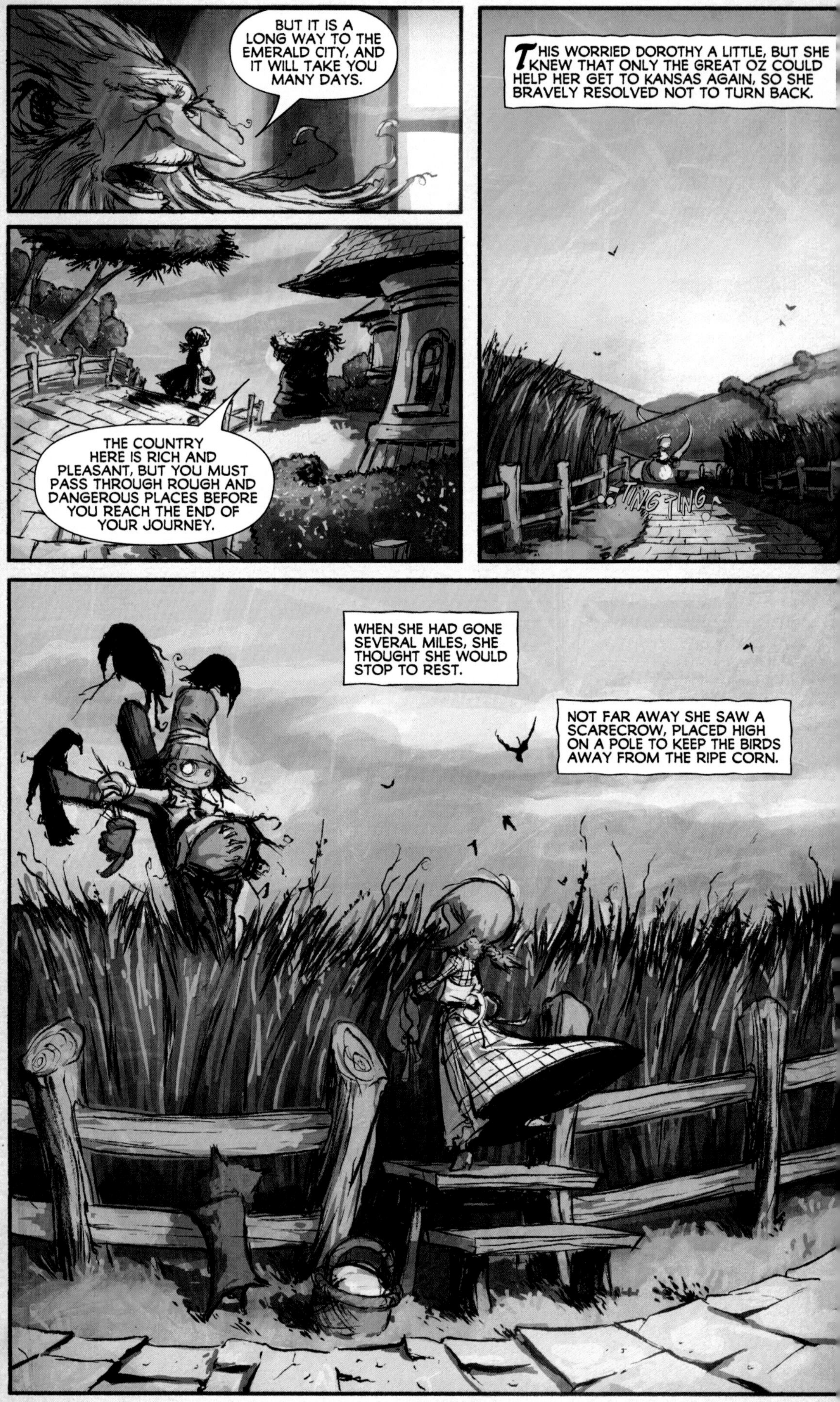
BUT IT IS A LONG WAY TO THE EMERALD CITY, AND IT WILL TAKE YOU MANY DAYS.
THE COUNTRY HERE IS RICH AND PLEASANT, BUT YOU MUST PASS THROUGH ROUGH AND DANGEROUS PLACES BEFORE YOU REACH THE END OF YOUR JOURNEY.
THIS WORRIED DOROTHY A LITTLE, BUT SHE KNEW THAT ONLY THE GREAT OZ COULD HELP HER GET TO KANSAS AGAIN, SO SHE BRAVELY RESOLVED NOT TO TURN BACK.
TING TING
WHEN SHE HAD GONE SEVERAL MILES, SHE THOUGHT SHE WOULD STOP TO REST.
NOT FAR AWAY SHE SAW A SCARECROW, PLACED HIGH ON A POLE TO KEEP THE BIRDS AWAY FROM THE RIPE CORN.

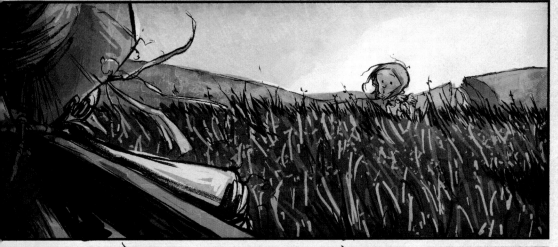

GOOD DAY.

Rowf! Rowf! Rowf!

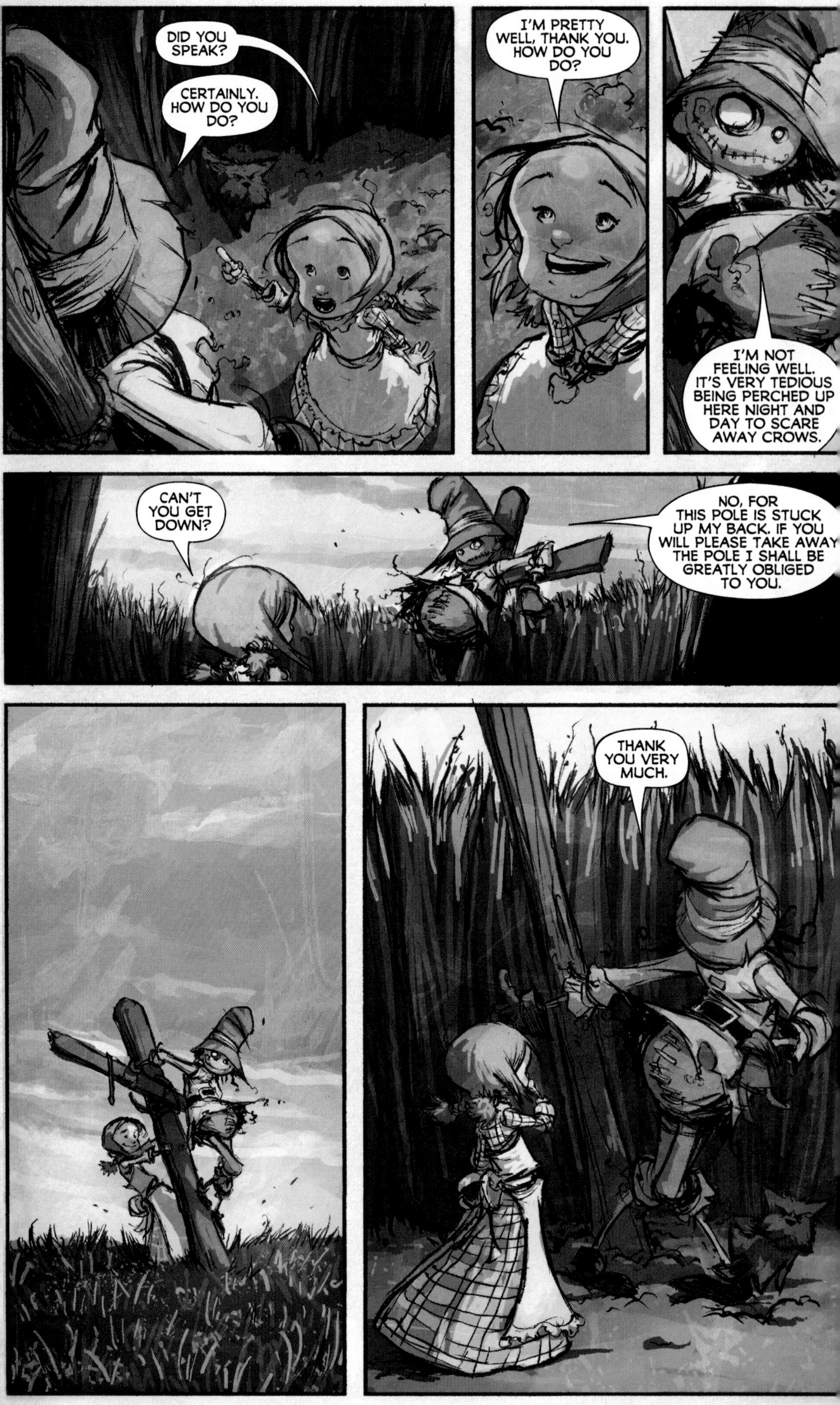
DID YOU SPEAK?
CERTAINLY. HOW DO YOU DO?
I'M PRETTY WELL, THANK YOU. HOW DO YOU DO?
I'M NOT FEELING WELL. IT'S VERY TEDIOUS BEING PERCHED UP HERE NIGHT AND DAY TO SCARE AWAY CROWS.
CAN'T YOU GET DOWN?
NO, FOR THIS POLE IS STUCK UP MY BACK. IF YOU WILL PLEASE TAKE AWAY THE POLE I SHALL BE GREATLY OBLIGED TO YOU.
THANK YOU VERY MUCH.

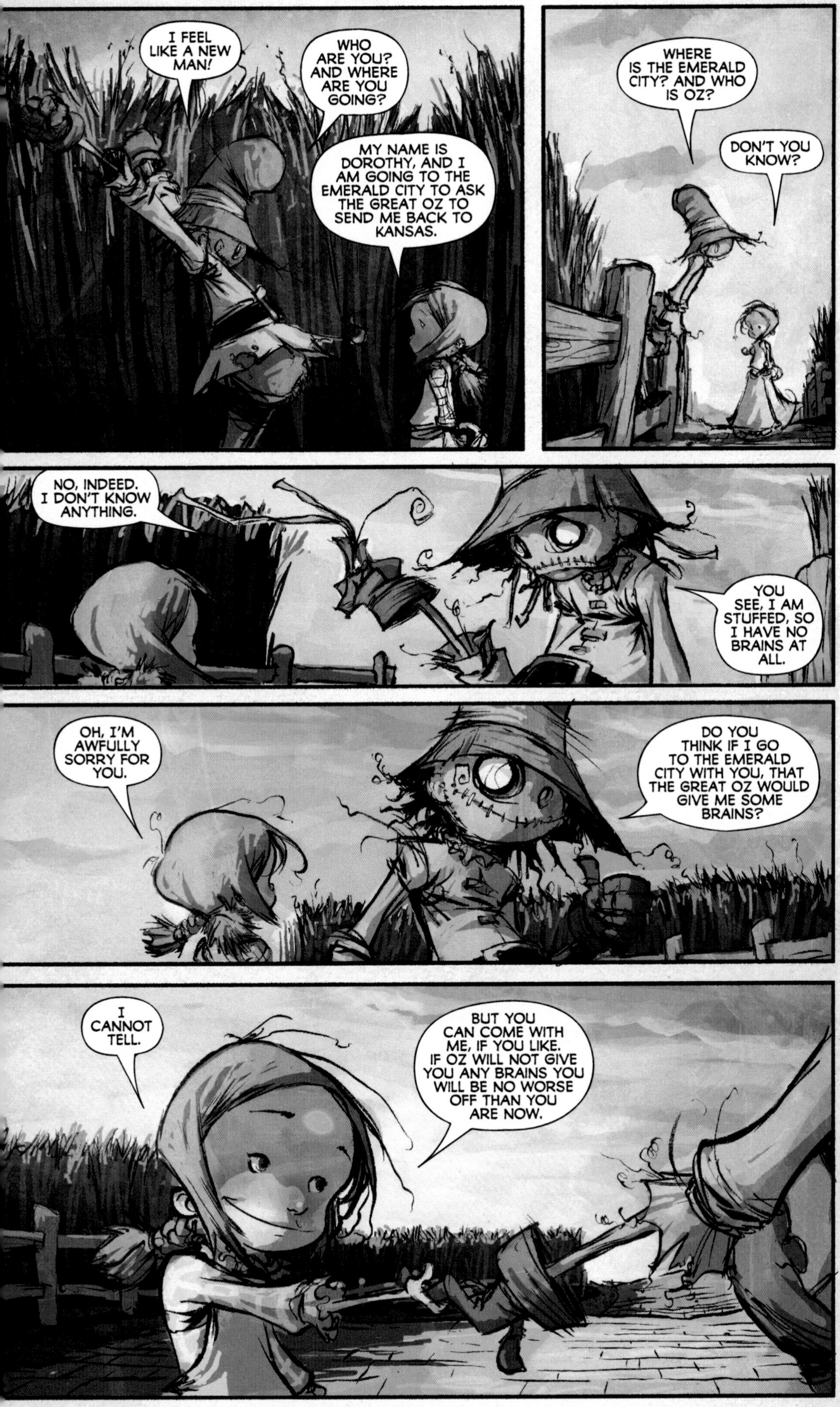

I FEEL LIKE A NEW MAN!
WHO ARE YOU? AND WHERE ARE YOU GOING?
MY NAME IS DOROTHY, AND I AM GOING TO THE EMERALD CITY TO ASK THE GREAT OZ TO SEND ME BACK TO KANSAS.
WHERE IS THE EMERALD CITY? AND WHO IS OZ?
DON'T YOU KNOW?
NO, INDEED. I DON'T KNOW ANYTHING.
YOU SEE, I AM STUFFED, SO I HAVE NO BRAINS AT ALL.
OH, I'M AWFULLY SORRY FOR YOU.
DO YOU THINK IF I GO TO THE EMERALD CITY WITH YOU, THAT THE GREAT OZ WOULD GIVE ME SOME BRAINS?
I CANNOT TELL.
BUT YOU CAN COME WITH ME, IF YOU LIKE. IF OZ WILL NOT GIVE YOU ANY BRAINS YOU WILL BE NO WORSE OFF THAN YOU ARE NOW.

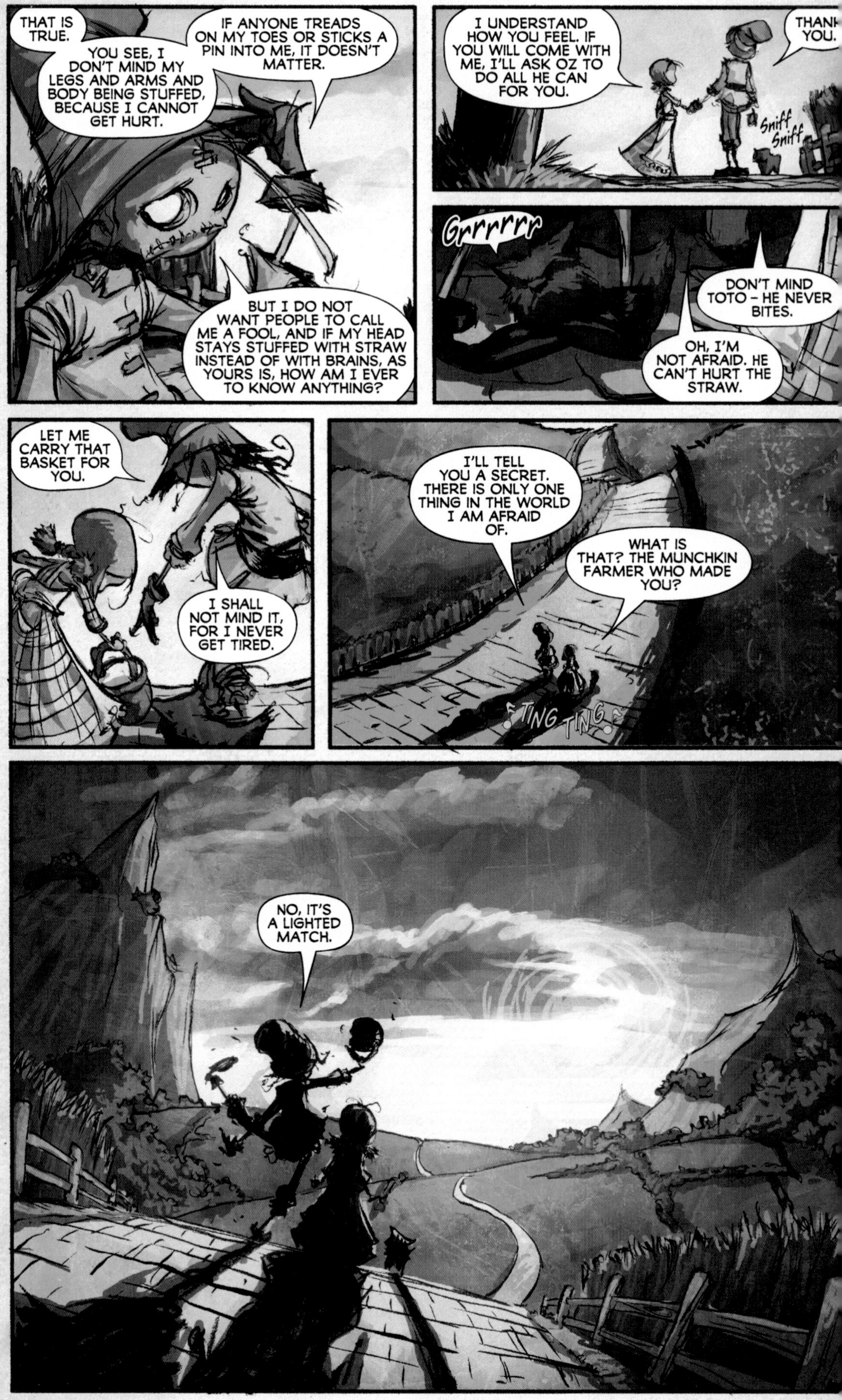
THAT IS TRUE.
YOU SEE, I DON'T MIND MY LEGS AND ARMS AND BODY BEING STUFFED, BECAUSE I CANNOT GET HURT.
IF ANYONE TREADS ON MY TOES OR STICKS A PIN INTO ME, IT DOESN'T MATTER.
BUT I DO NOT WANT PEOPLE TO CALL ME A FOOL, AND IF MY HEAD STAYS STUFFED WITH STRAW INSTEAD OF WITH BRAINS, AS YOURS IS, HOW AM I EVER TO KNOW ANYTHING?
I UNDERSTAND HOW YOU FEEL. IF YOU WILL COME WITH ME, I'LL ASK OZ TO DO ALL HE CAN FOR YOU.
THANK YOU.
Sniff Sniff
Grrrrrr
DON'T MIND TOTO – HE NEVER BITES.
OH, I'M NOT AFRAID. HE CAN'T HURT THE STRAW.
LET ME CARRY THAT BASKET FOR YOU.
I SHALL NOT MIND IT, FOR I NEVER GET TIRED.
I'LL TELL YOU A SECRET. THERE IS ONLY ONE THING IN THE WORLD I AM AFRAID OF.
WHAT IS THAT? THE MUNCHKIN FARMER WHO MADE YOU?
TING TING
NO, IT'S A LIGHTED MATCH.